Matthew Henson at the North Pole

CHARACTERS

Narrator 1	Amy
Narrator 2	Matt
Mrs. Morgan	Matthew Henson
Lori	Robert Peary
Hank	Ootah
Sue	Captain Bartlett

SETTING

A classroom and on an expedition to the North Pole

READER'S THEATER

Narrator 1: Mrs. Morgan's class is studying explorers.

Narrator 2: Right now they're talking about Matthew Henson and his trip to the North Pole. Let's listen in.

Mrs. Morgan: Matthew Henson was the first person to reach the North Pole and plant the American flag. Who knows when he did that?

Lori: I know. It was in the spring of 1909—April 6, I think.

Hank: But he started preparing for that historic moment long before that.

Sue: This wasn't his first trip, Mrs. Morgan.

Amy: He and Captain Peary had tried many times before.

Lori: But they always had to turn back because they ran out of food.

Mrs. Morgan: That's true. And on one trip in the spring, melting ice forced them to turn back.

Hank: In 1909, they made it all the way to the North Pole!

READER'S THEATER

Mrs. Morgan: Did you know they had been trying to reach the North Pole for 18 years?

Matt: Why is that such a big deal? Everybody knows what snow and ice look like.

Mrs. Morgan: Matt, don't you want to learn about one of our most famous explorers?

Matt: Gee, it's not as if he went to the Moon or someplace really cool like that.

Amy: But Matt, it's really cool at the North Pole. It's about 30 degrees below zero cool!

Hank: The North Pole is the most remote place on Earth. Those men were very brave to make that trip.

Lori: Right, Hank. Matt, did you know that no one ever tried to go to the North Pole by dogsled again?

Mrs. Morgan: Since then, people have flown over the North Pole or reached it by ship. But no one ever followed the same path that Matthew Henson and Robert Peary did. No one dared to.

Sue: Back then they didn't have airplanes to rescue them.

Amy: They couldn't call for help either!

READER'S THEATER

Matt: I still don't see what the big deal is.

Mrs. Morgan: You don't? Well then, Matt, I have an idea that might change your mind. Tomorrow I want you to report to the class on the legendary trip of Henson and Peary.

Matt: But Mrs. Morgan!

Mrs. Morgan: First thing tomorrow, Matt.

Narrator 1: At the end of the school day, the students in Mrs. Morgan's class went home.

Narrator 2: All except Matt, that is. He went to the library. He knew he had to do research to make his report.

Narrator 1: There was a whole shelf of books about Matthew Henson.

Matt: Maybe Matthew Henson was a big deal!

Narrator 2: Matt checked out several books. He went home and read and read…until he fell asleep and dreamed.

READER'S THEATER

Matt: Gosh, I'm cold. It's freezing! Why is it light outside? It's nighttime.

Henson: It's light in the Arctic almost all night in the summer. Just like it's dark all day in the winter.

Peary: We waited for the spring and the light. We spent six months in the fall and winter at our base camp. We made plans for the trip, and Matthew built sleds and hunted in the dark.

Matt: Who are you? Where am I?

Henson: You're part of our expedition to the North Pole.

Ootah: That's Matthew Henson and Captain Peary. I'm Ootah, Mr. Henson's native guide. That's Captain Bartlett. He's another explorer.

Matt: We're all alone out here?

Bartlett: There are four other explorers helping us. Each one did a leg of the trip and then turned back.

Ootah: Each one brought food and supplies and built a camp for the next one to use. That's how we've gotten this far.

Henson: It takes a lot of people to make a trip like this.

READER'S THEATER

Matt: I'm hungry. I want to go home!

Peary: Not yet, Matt. We might as well eat and get on our way again.

Ootah: Have some pemmican.

Matt: This is awful. What is this stuff?

Henson: It's dried walrus meat made into a powder and mixed with fat. I made it myself at base camp.

Bartlett: It's the only way to eat out here. Matthew is the best trapper and hunter. He's also a great cook!

Henson: On to the sleds, everyone. I want to keep away from the leads.

Matt: What are leads?

Peary: Leads are lanes of water made by melting ice. I fell into one a few days ago and almost died. Matthew Henson saved my life.

Bartlett: Matthew Henson has been with Captain Peary for 20 years. Before their Arctic explorations, they spent two years in Central America.

READER'S THEATER

Peary: There's no better Arctic explorer than Matthew. I depend on him for getting our food, handling the dogs and sleds, and using the compass. He even knows how to build igloos.

Ootah: Henson is a true friend of my people. He has learned our language, as well as our ways.

Bartlett: Better get going, men. I have to head back. Melting ice turned my igloo into an island floating out to sea. Good luck! I know you can make it!

Matt: I'll go back with you!

Peary: No, stay. We're getting close.

Henson: I tested the depth of the sea. It's more than 9,000 feet deep here. Shhh! Can you hear the ice cracking? More leads are opening.

Matt: Oh, no! I'm out of here! I'm waking up right now!

Narrator 1: And so he did.

Narrator 2: The next morning Matt rushed into Mrs. Morgan's classroom bursting with his news.

READER'S THEATER

Matt: Mrs. Morgan! Mrs. Morgan! I've changed my mind. I think Matthew Henson is an amazing explorer.

Mrs. Morgan: OK, Matt, slow down! Tell us why you think that.

Narrator 1: Matt told the class about the books he'd read and the dream he'd had. He talked about how hard the trip was. How cold it was. He described the melting ice and the Sun in the Arctic night.

Narrator 2: He explained how brave and smart Matthew Henson was.

Narrator 1: He reported that Matthew Henson and Captain Peary were the only ones to reach the North Pole.

Sue: Wow, Matt. What a story!

Lori: How did you know about the Sun being out all night in the summer?

Hank: Yeah. We didn't learn that in class, did we, Mrs. Morgan?

Mrs. Morgan: No. But Matt did a lot of reading last night. Perhaps that explains it. Or perhaps his dream made him think he was there.

Matt: Mrs. Morgan, trust me. I know I was. I can still feel the cold and taste the pemmican.

READER'S THEATER

All: Pemmican? What's that?

Matt: Dried walrus meat mixed with fat. It's really good.

All: Oh, yuck!

Matt: Did I do a good job on my report, Mrs. Morgan?

Mrs. Morgan: You did very well, Matt. Now, who wants to go to the Moon?

The End